Dusty and the Big Bad World

by Cusi Cram

A SAMUEL FRENCH ACTING EDITION

SAMUEL FRENCH

FOUNDED 1830

NEW YORK HOLLYWOOD LONDON TORONTO

SAMUELFRENCH.COM

ISBN 978-0-573-69691-6   Printed in U.S.A.   #29106

IMPORTANT BILLING AND CREDIT REQUIREMENTS

All producers of *DUSTY AND THE BIG BAD WORLD must* give credit to the Author of the Play in all programs distributed in connection with performances of the Play, and in all instances in which the title of the Play appears for the purposes of advertising, publicizing or otherwise exploiting the Play and/or a production. The name of the Author *must* appear on a separate line on which no other name appears, immediately following the title and *must* appear in size of type not less than fifty percent of the size of the title type.

In addition the following credit *must* be given in all programs and publicity information distributed in association with this piece:

DUSTY AND THE BIG BAD WORLD
had its world premiere in 2009
At The Denver Center Theatre Company,
Kent Thompson, Artistic Director

DUSTY AND THE BIG BAD WORLD had its world premiere with the Denver Center Theatre Company (Kent Thompson, Artistic Director) at The Space Theatre in Denver, Colorado, in January 23, 2009. It was directed by Kent Thompson, with scenic design by William Bloodgood, costume design by Bill Black, sound design by Jason Ducat, lighting design by Charles R. MacLeod, dramaturgy by Paul Walsh, and voice and dialect coaching by Kathryn G. Maes. The stage manager was Christi B. Spann, the assistant stage manager was Mr. Erock, the production manager was Edward Lapine, the production assistant was D. Lynn Reiland, and the production intern was Sarah Johnson. The cast, in order of appearance, was as follows:

JESSICA . . . . Kelly McAndrew

KAREN . . . . Jeanine Serralles

MARIANNE . . . . Charlotte Booker

NATHAN . . . . Sam Gregory

LIZZIE GOLDBERG-JONES . . . . Chloe Nosan

The understudies were Rob Hille (Nathan), Kate Hurster (Karen), Jordan Haleigh Morgan, (Lizzie Goldberg-Jones), Tracy Shaffer (Jessica, Marianne)

CHARACTERS

JESSICA – Early forties, driven, focused, a TV producer. Seemingly hard as nails but has a vulnerable side.

KAREN – Twenties, edgy, neurotic, was an addict, is barely keeping it together, is deeply self interested because she has to be – smarter than she lets on.

MARIANNE – Late-forties, early-fifties, Southern, very Christian, driven, seemingly soft but secretly hard as nails – has a super maternal side.

NATHAN – Late-thirties, early-forties, neurotic, wants to be heroic but it's not easy for him – becomes monomaniacal as the play progresses.

LIZZIE GOLDBERG-JONES – An honest, somewhat precocious 11 year-old – not an annoying kid. She speaks the truth more than anyone else in the play.

ACT ONE

(MARIANNE sits at a desk in an office in Washington D.C. She unpacks some folders from a box and laughs to herself.)

MARIANNE. I love my job. I know. I know it's not really alright to say that, not out loud. I could say it ironically, "I love my job," adding a whole other syllable to the word love. But that's not what I mean. Not at all.

In America – for the most part, people dislike their jobs but love the things their jobs give them – the actual stuff, the in-ground pool it finally buys, the many tiered pension plan – the freedom from a mortgage, or the ability to get an even bigger house and bigger mortgage that will never be paid off, no matter what job you get. It's so sad but so true.

People just love the illusion of freedom their jobs give them but they are not free precisely because they hate their work. They moan, they complain, they have heart attack after heart attack – always hating what they do. Not all people. But most.

I could shout that I love what I do off a roof top spinning in the wind – like some dope in a romantic comedy. And I don't do it for the money. Not at all. I love what I do. I keep this fact mostly to myself because I have learnt, learnt the hard way, to keep precious things close to my heart. But sometimes, sometimes, in spite of myself, it rushes forth – the love – it could be at a lecture to college students, or during an interview, or in the middle of a staff meeting. I feel it bubbling up, the ardor, the delight, the unqualified joy I take in my work.

MARIANNE. *(cont.)* I worry, I worry, I might seem smug or self-satisfied and THAT is NOT my intention, THAT is not a part of my agenda. I always want to appear humble, humble in the face of my happiness because I am. Truly so. And to appear any other way would be a fall, a fall from grace.

(**MARIANNE** *opens a box of pencils and inhales the erasers. Her assistant,* **KAREN** *enters and sees her. She turns on her heels.*)

KAREN. I…should go…call someone to fix the fax.

MARIANNE. You caught me.

KAREN. Sorry…there was a message on the voice…

MARIANNE. There is so much possibility in a box of new pencils. I've always felt that. Ever since I was a little girl in South Carolina.

KAREN. Yeah. Sure. Possibility.

MARIANNE. It's so thrilling setting up a new office. I never thought I would be sitting in THIS chair looking at THIS view.

KAREN. Well…you are…so…

MARIANNE. I'm excited. So excited, I'm inhaling my pencils like a third grader. Are you excited?

KAREN. *(not so excited)* Sure.

MARIANNE. The country spoke again and here we are continuing on with the work we started in 2001. I feel so blessed to be here today, on the brink…the brink of so much change. You seem like you feel blessed too, Karen.

KAREN. Sure.

MARIANNE. Try again, you didn't convince me.

KAREN. Well. I do. Really. I was unemployed for a long time…before…before I got this job. So I feel blessed… or rather thankful for the work. Work is…good.

MARIANNE. Exactly. We are engaged in good work, Karen. And THAT gets me up in the morning. THAT'S what I want to hear from people on my staff.

KAREN. What?

MARIANNE. Excuse me?

KAREN. What exactly do want to hear from your staff… so…I know? I mean…so…I think…I'm just confused. I'm sorry.

MARIANNE. You *never* have to be sorry for asking for clarification. Never. This is what I want to feel from my staff, Karen: that every day, every hour of every day, every minute of every hour, every second of every minute that they are ready to WORK to effect CHANGE.

KAREN. Well, I'm not here for the strippers. That just came out…oopsy.

MARIANNE. Oh Karen, you…you are chock 'o block full of wit and humor and that is why I hired you. Because… laughter, laughter is the best medicine. Right?

KAREN. Right. There was a message on your voice mail…

MARIANNE. Between you and me, I just can't believe I'm here, Karen. It hasn't sunk in, filtered through the system, settled into my DNA. There are a lot of places I could be working but I am HERE.

KAREN. You sure are. I see you.

MARIANNE. I have a view! A view of the Capitol!

KAREN. Oh, is that what that round building thingy is?

MARIANNE. Oh you! You! 'Tween you and me, I never dreamt this could happen. "The President's Special Counsel on Children and Child Welfare."

KAREN. Big title.

MARIANNE. Big job.

KAREN. Your title…it's kinda broad.

MARIANNE. EXACTLY. I have been given a wide berth, Karen. Wide. God bless the president and his dedicated staff for wanting to take such good care of the children of this land. I wanted my office to be here though, here in the Department of Education because that's where real transformation can happen for little ones…in school. If you set them on a sturdy moral path when they are young, mostly likely they'll continue on that path.

KAREN. Yeah. Sure. Education is…important…for kids and non kids.

MARIANNE. Oh, I have so many plans and dreams and wants for this job. We have so much to do Karen. We do. And I use the word "we" very consciously Karen, because I don't do anything alone, no one does of course, your opinions are as important to me as my own.

KAREN. I'll make a note of that.

MARIANNE. Do you have children Karen?

KAREN. God no.

MARIANNE. You're young. There's time. You are blessed with youth.

KAREN. Youth, overrated.

MARIANNE. Funny, funny. You. I appreciate your humor. I appreciate you, Karen.

*(An awkward pause. **KAREN** doesn't know if she should leave. **MARIANNE** fingers a picture of a little girl on her desk.)*

MARIANNE. This *is* Susanna. I use the present tense and sometimes that confuses people. Susanna was taken from me. But she's always with me. She's with me today Karen as we set up our office and get ready to make a real difference for children in this country.

*(**MARIANNE** looks at Susanna's picture.)*

KAREN. I'm sorry…about Susanna.

MARIANNE. Don't be sorry. It was the best thing that ever happened to me. Sometimes, I think everything I do for children, I do to protect her. If she were here, I'd probably be a stay at home Mom, driving her to soccer games, making her princess costumes and…big ole cakes. I'd have just one child. Now I have so many. God always has a plan for us, Karen. You said someone called.

*(**KAREN** hands **MARIANNE** a message slip.)*

KAREN. Terry Johnson, the president of PBS.

MARIANNE. If Mrs. Johnson ever calls again, Karen page me wherever I am, yell at the top of your lungs, yank me from the ladies. Is that clear?

KAREN. Crystal. But just for the record she called at six am. I like to work but not that much.

MARIANNE. You! You! Sharp as a tack, that's why you got the job. Get me Mrs. Johnson on the phone and a complete list of all children's programming produced under the Department of Ed's "Time to Teach" grants. That'll probably be filed under "diversity" and/or multi-cultural programming. Cancel my lunch appointment with the Secretary of Health and Human Services and reschedule for next Tuesday. And a coffee, two percent milk, two sweet and lows and two stirrers. It's time to stir things up, Karen.

(blackout)

(A different office in Cambridge Massachusetts. **JESSICA** *furiously types.* **NATHAN** *enters.)*

JESSICA. This is a disaster.

NATHAN. *(rapid fire)* EXACTLY! It's Batman and Robin and the McCarthy era all over again.

*(***JESSICA*** *rifles through a script.)*

JESSICA. Huh?

NATHAN. In the 40's a German psychiatrist wrote a fear mongering tome claiming that cartoons of men in tights living together would drive little boys to a life of sodomy.

JESSICA. Waaay to early for sodomy chat, Nathan.

NATHAN. A SENATE investigation followed of Batman and Robin, if you can believe it? Guess who was spearheading that little crusade?

JESSICA. No clue.

NATHAN. Jay Edgar Hoover and Roy Cohn. I rest my case.

JESSICA. What case?

NATHAN. I mean, even if Batman and Robin were sending crazy gay signifiers out to the universe – so what? Did the big conservative THEY really think that exposing little boys to robust, super-hero man love would somehow turn boys toward each other? You can't make someone gay, no matter how tight your tights are.

JESSICA. No idea. What. You are talking about. But Shirley's script sucks.

NATHAN. Oh my God, you haven't read Terry's e-mail! Read the e-mail, Jessica.

JESSICA. HOW is it possible for a writer to SUCK so profoundly?

NATHAN. That's not criticism, that's condemnation.

JESSICA. Have you read this…thing? It's talky, the dialogue is off, stakes are low, just…trim the fat.

*(***JESSICA*** *throws the script toward* **NATHAN.***)*

NATHAN. It's writing, not brisket.

JESSICA. Better yet, take the script away from her. Give it to Bill.

NATHAN. Jessica, she's the only woman we hired this season.

JESSICA. I think men are funnier.

NATHAN. You are so sexist.

JESSICA. On *this* particular show, on "Dusty." Men have the right edge.

NATHAN. You don't think women are edgy? You haven't met my wife.

JESSICA. The Dalai Lama would be edgy with three kids under five.

NATHAN. I'm not firing her.

JESSICA. Then make her script suck less.

(NATHAN *paces a little, thinking.*)

NATHAN. What can we do…what can we do to poor Shirley's script? We could, we could make Spuds allergic to radishes?

JESSICA. *(dead serious)* But Spuds is lactose intolerant! You know that!

NATHAN. Everyone on this show is allergic to something.

JESSICA. Because allergies are a HUGE kid issue.

NATHAN. Why is everyone so allergic? In my day peanut butter was not a dirty word. Is it the environment? Or some conspiracy with drug companies to secretly peck away at our immunity rendering us helpless without their drugs which cure us, while simultaneously making us perpetually allergic and in need of their semi-toxic drugs. What do you think?

JESSICA. Ok. Make Spuds AFRAID of radishes.

NATHAN. Are radishes scary?

JESSICA. Anything can be scary if it's unfamiliar to you. *(getting an idea)* OK. OK. We can play up the whole sub theme of the season: difference can be frightening but then you learn about it and PRESTO, it's less frightening. I don't know if radishes are the right lens for this story, maybe something more exotic? Yucca? Coconut?

NATHAN. I'll think of an appropriately scary vegetable or legume. Read the email from Terry. Seems she has some pretty McCarthy-esque views on "difference."

(JESSICA *reads her e-mail.* NATHAN *looks out the window.*)

NATHAN. Have you ever been snowshoeing? I think it might be peaceful. Less dangerous than skiing. *(beat)* I think I'm gonna take up snowshoeing. *(beat)* I'll never go snowshoeing.

(JESSICA *looks up from her e-mail.*)

JESSICA. OK.

NATHAN. I have a bad feeling about this. Like, I-could-lose-my-job, heads-are-going-to-roll feeling. I can't lose my job, Jessica.

JESSICA. You won't lose your job, Nathan.

NATHAN. I would be so royally fucked without this job. I mean, who would hire me?

JESSICA. People would hire you, Nathan.

NATHAN. What you're saying is I'm going to lose my job.

JESSICA. I'm saying, you have a definite skill set that is desirable in the current job market.

NATHAN. Yeah, I don't know about that. The actual skills of a producer/story editor are hard to describe. I write a little, edit a little, and try to translate your crushing comments to writers, so they can actually write.

JESSICA. This is a meeting about a show we produced with our boss – the head of PBS. That's all.

NATHAN. Did you read the same thing I did? Phrases like "gravely concerned" and "severe consequences for future funding" jumped out at me.
    Just when you think things can't get worse. They do. Get. Worse. Abu Ghraib. No WMD's. Fucker gets elected again. This.

JESSICA. Nathan, let's try to maintain some kind of perspective, here.

NATHAN. Oh, I think I have exactly the right perspective. Unbridled paranoia: appropriate response to our times.

That asshole stole another election by scaring ignorant Christians to the polls who usually don't vote by convincing them that gay people's right to marry would somehow endanger the moral fabric of their lives. Gay people don't live where those people live.

Roy Cohn? J Edgar Hoover? Puppies compared to Karl Rove and his league of Christian succubi. Give it another year and it's blacklist time.

JESSICA. Please. You're overreacting. You can never gauge tone from an e-mail.

NATHAN. But this was my little fiefdom of good, liberal values, Jessica. I could indoctrinate the next generation in our ways, so they wouldn't be forgotten.

JESSICA. We can still do that. Every day. We're safe, Nathan.

NATHAN. No one is safe. Not anymore. I really believed in that story.

JESSICA. It was a great idea AND it fit the mission of the grant – to promote diversity and different points of view.

NATHAN. I am so going to lose my job.

JESSICA. Everyone is vulnerable. We are a public organization – largely funded by the government. And our government SUCKS, more than Shirley's script, even.

NATHAN. The thing is, the thing is: I really liked that little girl.

JESSICA. She was chocolate in front of the camera.

NATHAN. She was vulnerable in all the right ways.

(blackout)

(Lights up on **LIZZIE**. *She speaks to a video camera.)*

LIZZIE. For the record: my favorite show is Sponge Bob. Sorry, it is. Do you guys watch that show? You should. Sponge Bob, he's like a sponge. He's supposed to be an underwater sponge but he looks like a dish washing sponge and he lives in a pineapple with his pet snail Gary and works as a fry cook at the Krusty Krab and has a really annoying neighbor, Squidward Tentacles who's like always taking bubble baths. *(***LIZZIE** *laughs, she snorts a little.)* That show rocks. Like sometimes it makes me laugh so hard I snort. Seriously.

My Dads like to watch the Gilmore Girls with us – they're really into the mother, Lorelei. I think she drinks way too much coffee and talks too fast. If my Dads talked that much, I'd put myself up for adoption. Honestly. I only watch it with them because we get to watch five hours of TV a week and because they watch the Gilmore Girls with me, it doesn't count because it's "family time." I love TV. My Dads say too much TV can make you dense as a Republican. They say that *all* the time.

I used to watch Dusty when I was little and it was OK. For the record: I don't watch it now and I only said I would enter this contest because my little brother Petey is obsessed with Dusty. He has Dusty sheets and PJs and can't go to sleep unless his two Dusty dust balls are tucked under each of his arms. I guess the whole idea of Dusty is kinda neat. I mean, it's cool that he's this dust ball and that he's made up of everything and everyone. And it's also kinda cool when he pulls some of himself off and then decides to go wherever that particle is from. But he travels in this magical dust-pan, which is a little lame, a dustpan? And his friend Spuds is lactose intolerant and that's ALL HE EVER TALKS ABOUT but whatever, the show is cool. I mean, if you're six. Petey is six.

So, when I heard the show had this competition, I thought, OK, why not? So. Dusty wants to know why he should come and visit us? Why we're special? I guess, first of all because Petey would love it more than anything in the world if you filmed us and then turned us into animated characters. It'd be like Sponge Bob – but not as cool. I also thought maybe if the kids at school saw. Petey on Dusty, saw my whole family animated – then maybe they would stop teasing Petey. It's not like he complains. But stuff bugs him. It bugs me too. People say the dumbest stuff, like it's really weird you have two Dads and the bible says this and that about gay people. And mostly I don't care about the bible or what other people say because we are agnostic Buddhists, anyway. But I thought if we were on TV then maybe people would stop saying stupid stuff. Because TV matters. It matters to everyone.

(Lights out on **LIZZIE**.*)*

(Lights up on **MARIANNE**. **MARIANNE** *sits at her desk talking to a picture of Susanna.)*

MARIANNE. I want to thank you for today. Today was a banner day, Susanna.

*(***KAREN** *enters.)*

You are my guide, my beacon through the darkness.

*(***MARIANNE** *notices* **KAREN**.*)*

KAREN. I'm sorry. Should I knock? Is that how you want to do it?

MARIANNE. Don't be silly. Mi oficina e tu oficina. Do you speak Spanish Karen?

KAREN. I speak no languages.

MARIANNE. Spanish is useful. If Susanna were still here, I would make sure she learnt Spanish.

KAREN. Yeah. Sure. Here's your schedule for tomorrow. It's pretty tight in the afternoon. I pushed back your meeting with the director of The Focus on Family.

MARIANNE. Did you have a good day today, Karen?

KAREN. There were no disasters, that's a good day for me.

MARIANNE. I like your style, Karen. I like your style, precisely because it's so different from my own.

KAREN. Thanks.

MARIANNE. Tell me Karen, do you watch public television?

KAREN. Well…at this particular point in time, I don't own a television – I hope to soon – but if I did have a TV, I think I would watch public television, yes.

MARIANNE. And why is that?

KAREN. Well…um first and foremost, there are no commercials.

MARIANNE. Exactly.

KAREN. Exactly what?

MARIANNE. There are no commercials because the "public" pays for programming. Here is my million dollar question for you Karen – do you think public television reflects the public it serves?

KAREN. Um…well…sure.

MARIANNE. I beg to differ. I think, for the last however many years, public television has served a very specific sector.

KAREN. And what sector would that be?

MARIANNE. Urban liberals, Karen.

KAREN. Right.

MARIANNE. I think we need to make public television more public, don't you?

KAREN. I'm not quite sure what that means.

MARIANNE. It means that if indeed public television is public, then it should reflect a wider demographic. If it doesn't then isn't it really "private" television?

KAREN. But…I forgot to backup the hard drive. Silly me.

MARIANNE. Please Karen, I value your opinion.

KAREN. Um…I guess…if "urban liberals" support public television then THEY can program whatever the heck they want. I mean they're the ones forking it over during those endless fund drives.

MARIANNE. True. Only thing is they don't wholly fund it, we, the government pick up a big chunk of the tab.

KAREN. It seems like society has worse ills than PBS. I mean, did Masterpiece Theater ever scar someone for life?

MARIANNE. I'm not talking about Masterpiece Theater.

KAREN. I guess I'm not clear what you're talking about.

MARIANNE. Here's a juicy tidbit: a huge source of revenue for PBS is the profits they make off of merchandise associated with their children's programming.

KAREN. Silly me, that's where the Special Counsel on Children and Child Welfare comes in.

MARIANNE. With bells ringing.

KAREN. But I mean, just playing devil's advocate, or rather…whatever…PBS programs good television for kids – if such a thing exists.

MARIANNE. I think television can be instructive and informative and an excellent tool in early childhood development.

KAREN. I mean, who's gonna complain about Sesame Street?

MARIANNE. I have a bone or two to pick with that show. It caters exclusively to an urban demographic.

KAREN. But...but...there are a lot of kids in cities.

MARIANNE. Of course there are. But there are also children who live in suburbs and exurbs and in the middle of fields and trees and that particular show does not take those children and their specific belief systems into account.

KAREN. But I love Sesame Street! Kermit saved my life.

MARIANNE. And how did he do that?

KAREN. Oh. I had this thing about him when I was a kid. I only wore green socks all through second grade, which was a particularly tough time for me, messy divorce, custody battle...whatever. So, if anyone teased me, I looked at my socks and whispered to myself, "it's not easy being green." So much more than you need to know.

MARIANNE. You've proven my point.

KAREN. I didn't mean to...I mean...what point?

MARIANNE. That what children watch on television when they are young is highly influential. Now don't you worry, Karen, Kermit and all his little urban friends are not my current area of focus.

KAREN. Would you mind my asking who is?

MARIANNE. A certain animated dust ball.

KAREN. Dusty! My niece loves that show.

MARIANNE. Not for long.

KAREN. Did Dusty misbehave?

MARIANNE. You could say that Dusty is a deviant.

KAREN. Sounds intriguing...I mean complicated.

MARIANNE. If I have my way, and I usually do, Karen, Dusty and all his lucrative merchandise is about to become...

KAREN. Dust.

MARIANNE. You said it.

KAREN. You certainly are starting with a bang.

MARIANNE. I didn't plan to but sometimes God hands you the unexpected on a Chippendale platter.

KAREN. My surprises usually materialize on plastic.

MARIANNE. Funny, funny.

KAREN. True, true.

MARIANNE. It's great to have you on my team, Karen.

KAREN. Yeah it's good to be…on a team? Is there anything else?

MARIANNE. Go ahead and distribute the memo I sent you. I am more than done for the day.

(KAREN exits. MARIANNE looks at the photograph of Susanna. Blackout.)

(KAREN at a pay phone. She looks both ways and dials a number. It rings. Lights up on NATHAN in his office. The phone rings. NATHAN picks the phone up.)

NATHAN. *(curt)* I promise you I will pick up baby wipes and the pâté, honey. I have it written down on my hand. *(writing on his hand)* There's this major shit storm happening at work so could you lay off for ten minutes.

KAREN. Hello?

NATHAN. I'm so, so sorry. This is Nathan Friedman. And I don't always talk to my wife like that.

KAREN. I know.

NATHAN. Excuse me?

KAREN. I mean, I know who you are. You're a producer of Dusty, right?

NATHAN. And this is the point in the conversation where you introduce yourself.

KAREN. Look, you need to come to Washington and meet me.

NATHAN. You sound very nice but I'm married with three kids and I still don't know your name.

KAREN. It's better if you don't. This is serious. I work for the government. And there are people, people who um…they don't have your best interests at heart.

NATHAN. Me specifically? Someone in the government wants to kill me?

KAREN. The show, the show, they want to kill the show. Meet me at the Au Bon Pain in Union Station tomorrow at 7:30 p.m.

NATHAN. This is very weird, very Deep Throat, except I'm not a journalist. I wanted to be a journalist.

KAREN. I have an incriminating memo.

NATHAN. Who does it incriminate?

KAREN. Someone very important – someone at the top.

NATHAN. At PBS?

KAREN. At the mothership. Let's just say someone there is sleeping with the enemy.

NATHAN. Who? And who is the mothership? And what do you want from me? I think up stories about saintly dust balls with allergic Bunny friends. I need more information.

KAREN. I can't talk. Tomorrow. The Au Bon Pain. Union Station. 7:30 p.m.

NATHAN. Can't we meet at a bar?

KAREN. *(vehemently)* NO BARS. The Au Bon Pain or nowhere.

NATHAN. Well, maybe I don't go to Au Bon Pains, maybe I oppose their version of the croissant?

KAREN. There is a very small window of time here. My boss is like a forest fire.

NATHAN. Listen, my life is very complicated, mystery lady…

KAREN. 7:30. Union Station. Au Bon Pain. And keep this under your hat.

(The sound of a dial tone. Lights out on KAREN. NATHAN looks confused. JESSICA sticks her head in NATHAN's office.)

JESSICA. You ready for tomorrow morning?

NATHAN. For the wrath of Terry Johnson? How does one prepare?

JESSICA. It'll be fine, Nathan.

NATHAN. Fine like Guantanamo is fine?

JESSICA. What you need is a glass of white wine and a Valium.

(JESSICA hands NATHAN a little pack of Valium.)

NATHAN. I feel beyond Valium.

(He takes the Valium.)

JESSICA. Hey, LOVED the whole lima bean beat. Good choice of a familiar yet slightly exotic legume.

NATHAN. Different but not TOO different. Right down the middle.

JESSICA. Come on, we don't play it safe. Remember last year when Dusty met that Muslim…what was it?

NATHAN. It was supposed to be a hedgehog but it looked more like a rat, which I, personally, don't think did much for Arab/American relations.

JESSICA. More like a mole than a rat.

NATHAN. That was last year. This year it's another country. You can't be fine with this meeting.

JESSICA. I am fine with this meeting. And thanks for making Shirley's script fly – I didn't think it was possible.

NATHAN. It's my job.

JESSICA. And you do it superbly, Nathan.

(JESSICA *exits.*)

NATHAN. Not for long, if Terry Johnson has her way.

(*blackout*)

(**MARIANNE** *packs up her briefcase and is about to leave. Her phone rings. She picks it up.*)

MARIANNE. Marianne Fitzgibbons, how may I be of service? Terr – iii! How is my most favorite Kappa Kappa Delt? So you got the MEMO. Uh huh. Uh Huh. Uh Huh. Sure thing Terr – iii, sweet pea. It is bold. No shrinking violet am I. You know and I know, that little girl should not have been chosen from a national contest and bless her it's not her fault she was. It's called "public television" not "special interest television that caters to people with alternative lifestyles not sanctioned by all the major religions in the entire world" television. You're with me there…right?

I hear you, baby, I know I am putting you in a tight spot. But I've never cared for that show…the main character Dusty…well…he seems a little too tolerant of just about everything and I know he is an inanimate object but honey, he seems like a homosexual dust ball to me. There, I said it.

Listen sweet thing, I know…I know that your concern was the episode. We can discuss the future of the show in more detail at a later date. But bottom line, they misused government funds and there has to be con-sequences. Action, reaction, it's a law of physics AND politics. Right. Right. Right.

Terry, people at the top, at the very tippy top will be ever so grateful if you…well if you stay flexible and open to suggestions. This administration is very open to like-minded women. If you catch my drift. (*beat*) Sounds like you caught it. I am going to do my Kappa Kappa Delta best to make sure that YOU get the lion's share of credit for this. Oh yeah…he got the MEMO too. EVERYONE got the memo…your little sorority sister is starting with a BANG.

Sweetie, I'm running beyond late, Frank'll have my head. He's cookin a ham. Ham, that's right. I know I can count on you, Terry. God bless you too.

(**MARIANNE** *hangs up the phone.*)

(*fiercely*) YES!

(The next day. JESSICA *sits at her desk and shakes a sugar packet before putting it into her Starbucks coffee.* NATHAN *watches her. She shakes a another packet.* NATHAN *can't take his eyes off of her. He holds a coffee cup in his hands but doesn't drink it.)*

JESSICA. *(stirring)* We're behind on 213B. They need to start storyboarding next week. When are we taping voices?

NATHAN. Uh...

JESSICA. The twelfth. I think it's the twelfth.

NATHAN. The twelfth...yeah...that sounds like...a number...Can I have some sugar?

*(*JESSICA *hands him some sugar packets. He puts the coffee on her desk and pours packet after packet of sugar in his coffee.* JESSICA *notices.)*

JESSICA. Sweet tooth's calling?

NATHAN. Yelling. I guess I don't understand...

JESSICA. I can go over the notes but I thought I was pretty clear – I just don't buy the B story with the goblin. Dusty can't be afraid for no reason. That's part of his charm...his universality. He is made of everything, therefore nothing is that foreign to him. AND the goblin doesn't seem real to me.

NATHAN. The goblin doesn't seem real to you? Well, none of this...this day...the meeting we just had and you... you shaking sugar into your Starbucks coffee as if it's just a day, like every other day where you shake the sugar – none of it seems the least bit real to me, Jessica.

JESSICA. I think the meeting went well, Nathan.

NATHAN. OK what you just said is more unreal than an animated goblin who is familiar but not familiar who doesn't seem real.

JESSICA. The meeting went well, because we're not going to lose the show. You have to trust me, Nathan.

NATHAN. But I don't.

JESSICA. What?

NATHAN. I mean, I get it...I do...You created Dusty...
I mean you didn't create him but you lifted him up
and out of the world of obscure children's literature
and put him on lunch boxes and knapsacks and you...
whipped up a world of little fluffy toys...but...

JESSICA. The show is a hit because we bust our asses making
accessible but complicated stories for children and the
lunch boxes and toys followed.

NATHAN. No, I know. I'm saying you made a good...some
might even say great, show. And I helped you and I
can understand wanting to hold on to that. But I can't
help feeling...feeling that you hung me out to dry in
that meeting to save some...some inflated notion of
your purpose....

JESSICA. I thought we were in that room as a team.

NATHAN. Yeah...um...not a team I want to be on.

JESSICA. I was being diplomatic.

NATHAN. You were being sycophantic.

JESSICA. I was...surveying, surveying is very different from
sycophanting.

NATHAN. You waffled...you balked...you gave up, Jessica.

JESSICA. Hardly, I decided to fight.

NATHAN. It didn't look like you were fighting.

JESSICA. Exactly, that was exactly my plan. Terry is my boss,
she has the power to green light or kill all of our best
ideas. So, if she has concerns about a show we made, I
damn well better listen to her concerns.

NATHAN. Well...Terry Johnson doesn't seem to think gay
parents should appear on children's television.

JESSICA. That's not what she said. She had some interesting
points...

NATHAN. None...none of them were interesting.

JESSICA. Her point about whether it's really the job of television to educate children about homosexuality had
some merit.

NATHAN. Yes. Yes, it is our job.

JESSICA. *I* can't say that I know that for a fact.

NATHAN. You would if you had children.

JESSICA. I am perfectly capable of making judgments about what children should or shouldn't know without having any of my own. AND my seven Emmys would seem to indicate that my knowledge of children's needs and likes is quite expert.

NATHAN. I think Terry Johnson and what she thinks children should and shouldn't know...is wacko. Kids... they are not these sacred little beings...our job is to educate them about the world...the complexity, hardship and beauty of it all not pretend that everyone is just like them and that – yipee – isn't that hunky dory.

JESSICA. I think Terry's views are more complex than that.

NATHAN. What about *your* views, Jessica?

JESSICA. My views are not the issue at this particular moment. You know and I know, that without the profits from Dusty lunch boxes there would be no Nova. No Frontline.

NATHAN. Not sure how much Frontline matters in the world we live in, Jessica. Unless they're planning a show about Karl Rove's use of bigotry and fear to control the minds of America's under educated electorate.

JESSICA. Nathan, I can't be angry all the time about everything.

NATHAN. But you have to be angry about THIS. This is a complete infringement of the First Amendment, Jessica.

JESSICA. I just don't view it that way. Look, I need to keep Dusty on the air and by doing that fund the three other programs I'm developing. If we lose the show, you know and I know, the whole network could...disappear....same way the Clinton surplus did.

NATHAN. Good luck with those shows. The way things are going, I think you'll be creating a sweet show about a little boy named Jesus whose Mom is so magical she didn't have to have sex to conceive him.

JESSICA. Terry had *specific* concerns about introducing the issue of homosexuality on a *specific* show.

NATHAN. But the episode was about a *family* not about homosexuality. And Lizzie's Dad's are married. It's not like they're living in "sin." /I don't even know what that means.

JESSICA. //I know they're married, Nathan.

NATHAN. Where do you stand on gay marriage, Jessica?

JESSICA. Come on.

NATHAN. I am not sure after that meeting where you stand on anything.

JESSICA. I'm pro everything you are, gay marriage, a women's right to choose, electric cars, never using a plastic bag or bottle again. *(beat)* Why am I doing this? I don't have to do this.

NATHAN. So, you're just going to sit back and let them cancel the episode?

JESSICA. Would you show it to your children, Nathan?

NATHAN. In a heartbeat.

JESSICA. Why?

NATHAN. Because the Goldberg-Jones are a fun and loving family and I want my children to see families different from their own.

JESSICA. We have to be sensitive to *all* our viewers. We owe them that.

NATHAN. Oh my God, it's like they got to you in the night and injected you with some "Doubting Christian" serum.

JESSICA. Can you try not to be ridiculous for one second. I think the whole episode was a misjudgment on my part.

NATHAN. No it wasn't.

JESSICA. If it hadn't been part of a national contest, if we hadn't gotten 15,000 video submissions. Maybe we stretched the meaning of the word diversity. The mission of the grant was to promote ethnic and religious diversity. Sexual diversity is a whole other kettle of fish.

NATHAN. Lizzie and her family are agnostic Buddhists. Not religiously diverse enough for you?

JESSICA. Believe me, I don't enjoy being in this position, Nathan.

NATHAN. But you are, Jessica, you are and now is the moment to fight, to scream from rooftops, to bully every PBS affiliate to air the show. What will happen if we do, will every child in America suddenly boycott their heterosexual parents in favor of Gay ones?

JESSICA. I'm trying to navigate something far bigger than myself, Nathan.

NATHAN. Well so is Lizzie Goldberg Jones. What are we telling her? We're telling her that it's not OK to be her.

JESSICA. I'll call her.

NATHAN. It's not a call.

JESSICA. You're right. I'll drive out and see her.

NATHAN. No...I will.

JESSICA. You don't have to, Nathan.

NATHAN. Yes I do. I do because I believe in her and her amazing parents and her pet pig and her little brother who does ballet. I believe in the way she conducts her life. And I want her to know that even though the President of PBS thinks she's a freak not worthy of air time – I think she's A-number-1 and I wish she was on my TV 24/7.

(a moment)

NATHAN. *(beat)* I just want to...to do good work, Jessica.

JESSICA. And you do. Sometimes, you have to compromise to keep doing good things. I am going to save Dusty. And by saving Dusty, I'm saving the 2 percent profit that we make on all the products he generates. And that money will save this network from complete and utter obsolescence. I just can't air Lizzie's episode and do it.

(a pause)

NATHAN. I gotta go…go to Washington.

JESSICA. Washington?

NATHAN. A friend. Friend with marriage troubles…

JESSICA. I hope he's OK.

NATHAN. Yeah…he wants to meet in an Au Bon Pain.

JESSICA. Sounds dire.

NATHAN. Yup.

JESSICA. And don't worry. I'm going to fight for your job, Nathan.

NATHAN. I'm not sure I want it anymore.

(blackout)

(The Au Bon Pain at Union Station. **NATHAN** *sits at a table and smokes. He looks bleary and un-tucked.* **KAREN** *enters. She is bundled up in a large scarf and a wool cap. She sees* **NATHAN** *who blows a smoke ring. She looks both ways and approaches the table.)*

KAREN. Put out the cigarette.

NATHAN. Excuse me?

KAREN. You can't smoke in here.

NATHAN. No one else seems to mind.

KAREN. I mind.

*(***KAREN*** *takes the cigarette and stomps it on the floor. She picks up the butt, doesn't quite know what to do with it and ends up stuffing it in her purse.)*

NATHAN. Are you my contact?

KAREN. Yes.

NATHAN. I'm Nathan.

KAREN. I know.

NATHAN. What should I call you?

KAREN. Uh…I don't know.

NATHAN. I need to call you something.

KAREN. You smell like a hobo.

NATHAN. I was early and availed myself of a few Johnny Walkers at the local TGIF, which I might add has a lot more personality than this place.

KAREN. *(fiercely)* I am not going to a bar! Look, I don't have a lot of time.

NATHAN. You're very bundled up for October.

*(***KAREN*** *sits. She unfurls her very long scarf and looks both ways.)*

NATHAN. Can I call you Madame O?

KAREN. Call me…Peg. You can call me Peg.

NATHAN. But I don't like the name Peg.

KAREN. Please…you have to FOCUS.

NATHAN. I'm sorry. I've had a helluva day.

KAREN. Yeah…well every day is a helluva day for me.

NATHAN. Sorry. I'm pulling myself together. Honest. I could use a coffee.

KAREN. No time for coffee.

NATHAN. Yes Sir! Peg Sir! No coffee, Sir.

(KAREN *opens her bag and pulls out a piece of paper and hands it to* NATHAN. *He tries to read it and then realizes he need his glasses. He fumbles around looking for his glasses.* KAREN *is about to explode.*)

KAREN. Jesus!

NATHAN. *(putting on his glasses)* Sorry.

(NATHAN *reads. He puts down the piece of paper.*)

NATHAN. That certainly sobered me up. Who wrote this?

KAREN. Give it back.

NATHAN. Can I get a copy of this?

KAREN. Absolutely not.

(KAREN *pulls the paper out of* NATHAN*'s hands.*)

NATHAN. Who do you work for exactly…Peg?

KAREN. I can't say.

NATHAN. But someone pretty high up?

KAREN. You could say that.

NATHAN. Someone in the administration.

KAREN. Yes. My boss is employed by this administration.

NATHAN. Wow. How do you do it?

KAREN. What?

NATHAN. Work for the anti-Christ I mean…technically I suppose you're working for Christ – just a strange unloving, version of the Messiah…or rather a Messiah who loves very conditionally. How do you sleep at night, Peg?

KAREN. Fuck you. I have a job, OK. I need a job. And a job can just be a job.

NATHAN. Sorry. I understand. I do. I am almost positive after reading that memo, I will not have a job and I have three kids and a wife who loves to shop...like all the time...shopping is her church...so I know what a job can mean.

KAREN. You...know what a job can mean...People assume a lot. They assume a lot about you because maybe you have hip shoes and a hand-knitted hat and you seem like you have half a brain...they assume that you can just make a living....that you can have your own life and pay your bills and THAT is a big assumption. These shoes are four years old...catch my drift?

NATHAN. No.

KAREN. Let's just say hypothetically....you are a college-educated white woman, working toward a masters degree in something arty – something arty but with some sort of practical application in the workplace. Let's say – hypothetically that you are a part time graphic design student and you work part time in a restaurant and your life is on course, you have goals, desires and just a little bit of talent, which is all anyone really needs to succeed in this great land of ours.

All is well, you are well, and then BOOM you hit a rough patch emotionally. Let's say you find your boyfriend sleeping with your younger, barely legal HOT sister and let's say you kinda fall apart.

You stop paying bills, you stop going to classes, you make it to your part-time job because you need cash, you don't have a rich family or brother, or grandma in the wings, in fact, your whole family is financially irresponsible and barely scraping by in parts of the country you have no desire to ever live in, like Central Florida, for example.

One day, you awaken at 10 am and let's say you take your morning Tylenol P.M. You have your two glasses of cheap morning Chardonnay with some cold pizza and you realize that you don't have enough white wine or Tylenol P.M to get through the day and it will be a

KAREN. *(cont.)* long day as your job at an upscale eatery in Georgetown doesn't begin 'til 5 p.m. You get in the car to drive to the Strip mall where, as luck would have it, there is a CVS AND a package store that sells your particular brand of New York State chardonnay.

Here's the HITCH in your plan. The STITCH in your side. The foil to your foggy state of mind – Somehow as you are driving in your car, listening to, let's say, some trance music you love, DESPITE the fact that your bone-headed ex gave it you – you run through a red light and then in an INSTANT you wake up. You wake up BIG TIME.

The EDGE is in your face. You are at one with the edge. You might even say as the paramedics scrape you and the other people in the four cars that have spun out of control, simply because you were listening to a cool beat and thinking about your morning high, you have BECOME the edge.

And things, let's say things get more complicated, the really complicated thing is that you have not paid your car insurance in two months and it has been canceled on that very day, that very exact day, hypothetically that is.

Suddenly, your life is not your own anymore, your life belongs to six people who have various internal and skeletal injuries and want to sue your ass off. Let's say and all this is very hypothetical of course, things get even more complicated when you are given a blood alcohol test and your levels are through the roof, because in fact you have been drunk for three months. You barely sleep, despite the Tylenol P.M. What you do is drink.

Somehow, through a stream of events which involve rehab and going on welfare and avoiding prison time by taking a vaguely Christian life-skills program at a local community center, you find yourself offered a job at the White House. Lets say you are offered this job because the woman who runs the vaguely Christian life

KAREN. *(cont.)* skills program has a very, very dear friend who works for the President and that very same woman with the important job believes in giving people second chances because...though it is never stated boldly and clearly in capital letters she had SOME DARKNESS IN HER PAST.

In fact, because you are white and college educated and not addicted to crack she decides to give you a pretty important job with lots of responsibility at least for someone like you – the new "fallen" you.

And because, let's say, you have been truly humbled by life and have done a lot of twelve stepping, you are filled with a deep gratitude to your new, strange Christian boss and have begun to believe that your life may some day be your own again, even though it is not for one second the life you imagined yourself having but it's a lot better than the other lives you have lived since that fateful moment at the intersection – that moment when you became the edge.

Despite your dreams of fame, fulfilment and having a HOT husband and a HOT career, you have become someone who is simply grateful for a JOB, hypothetically speaking that is.

NATHAN. Uh...Wow. What are you doing here...Peg?

KAREN. She dissed Sesame Street.

NATHAN. Oh.

KAREN. I feel like there are very few things that you can point to in life and feel certain that they are intrinsically good.

NATHAN. True.

KAREN. People let you down...well they let me down. Not Sesame Street. Sesame Street never let me down.

NATHAN. Peg, you're very noble. A muppet warrior.

KAREN. I'm an addict. I'm completely self-absorbed.

NATHAN. Well then...what's in it for you?

KAREN. Sleep. I can't take any kind of sedatives. And when you said earlier how do you sleep at night. I don't.

NATHAN. Alright, then.

KAREN. I thought I could take this job and just be fine with it. *(beat)* What next?

NATHAN. We should leak that memo to the press.

KAREN. OK, first off, there is no WE in this endeavor. Secondly, they would trace it directly back to me. Only a very few people have access to that kind of internal stuff.

NATHAN. It's just…I'm paranoid by nature, my boss thinks I'm a live wire as it is if…I tried to insinuate…what's in that memo…without any proof, no one would listen. I'd just be another paranoid, screaming liberal, which in fact I am.

(KAREN gets up and starts putting on her scarf.)

KAREN. This was a big mistake.

(NATHAN stands.)

NATHAN. No it wasn't. It wasn't a mistake. Information is always good.

KAREN. Is it?

NATHAN. Yes. Sit. Please.

(KAREN sits.)

NATHAN. How does your boss know Terry Johnson?

KAREN. Sorority sisters.

NATHAN. You work for Margaret Spellings?

KAREN. Worse.

NATHAN. Ok. *(beat)* Not that Child Welfare monstrosity? I thought. I thought when I saw her on TV at her swearing in, practically spooning Cheney, I thought, she is somehow going to fuck my world.

KAREN. Yeah, well. You were right.

NATHAN. Will they never stop? Shit. Omygod. Omygod. Fuck! We have to leak this memo. NOW! It'll completely outrage the left – public radio and TV is our version of crack.

KAREN. No leaks. No WE. Just let people know at work that government has an agenda…that isn't in their best interest.

NATHAN. I think they're already aware of that, Peg. Your boss wants to put an end to government funding of public television for children until it reflects a more "palatable ideology," I believe were her mindbendingly horrific words, which by the way, means ALL public television, 'cause the pastel-colored cartoons and fuzzy puppets with googly eyes keep Bill Moyers in fair trade coffee.

You'll find another job. Peg, you've put yourself in a position to do something really important in relation to the culture wars that are going on in this country.

KAREN. I don't want to be involved in any kind of war.

NATHAN. You already are involved.

KAREN. Unwillingly.

NATHAN. You called me.

KAREN. Because I want YOU to do something about this.

NATHAN. Listen, we sometimes do things and we don't know why. But great good can come out of sudden impulses.

KAREN. Do you have some heartbreaking story you're going to tell me from your life?

NATHAN. No.

KAREN. I am sooo relieved.

NATHAN. You are here for a reason. And so am I.

KAREN. That's your third Johnny Walker talking. I leaked you some information. That's it.

(KAREN *gets up.*)

NATHAN. That can't be it. There must be more. Please Peg. Pretty please. This is HUGE, you know it is or you wouldn't have called me.

KAREN. Fuck! Will nothing ever be simple again! *(beat)* I need time to think.

NATHAN. You don't need to think. You need to just act, lash out, fucking bring down this administration.

KAREN. What are you like when you're sober?

NATHAN. Worse.

KAREN. I gotta get to a meeting.

NATHAN. Peg!

KAREN. It's part of my parole. I'll call you.

(**KAREN** *wraps her long scarf around her neck.*)

NATHAN. Good to meet you, Peg.

KAREN. Get a cup of coffee.

(**KAREN** *looks both ways and begins to walk off.*)

NATHAN. Call me, Peg! You owe it to your country.

(**KAREN** *looks over her shoulder at* **NATHAN.**)

You owe it to yourself.

(*blackout*)

(**MARIANNE**'s office. *The next evening.* **MARIANNE** *packs up her laptop. The phone rings.* **MARIANNE** *picks it up.*)

MARIANNE. Hello, dear. I'm leaving right now. I promise. Oh, yes that sounds just delicious.

(**KAREN** *stands in the doorway with a file.* **MARIANNE** *motions for her to come in.*)

MARIANNE. I think apricots with chicken wrapped in Canadian bacon sounds yummy. I'll pick up some more bacon. And some more apricots. Promise. I do too, Bunny-man.

(**MARIANNE** *puts down the phone.*)

MARIANNE. My husband. He took a French cooking class. Good for him, not so good for my waist line.

KAREN. I thought you might want this.

MARIANNE. *(looking at the file)* Oh, yes, thank you Karen that's very thoughtful.

KAREN. You're welcome, Marianne.

MARIANNE. I hope you have a restful weekend.

KAREN. Yeah…

MARIANNE. I hope to do some gardening. Do you have some hobbies you look forward to pursuing on the weekends?

KAREN. Uh…hobbies? I mean, sometimes I draw.

MARIANNE. But that's more than a hobby for you. Your background is in the visual arts, isn't it?

KAREN. Kind of.

MARIANNE. I find raking, planting, pulling up weeds to be very relaxing. Nature doesn't ask for anything.

KAREN. Yeah.

(**KAREN** *begins to go. She turns around.*)

KAREN. I don't have a garden…or any hobbies, really.

MARIANNE. Well, maybe you should spend a little time in the park this weekend. The trees are turning, should be beautiful.

KAREN. I hate parks. I don't hate them but I hate the crowds. There's always someone with a boom box or a screaming baby that interrupts your thoughts...or your view of...a bird...or leaves or whatever.

MARIANNE. Yes, parks can sometimes be very challenging.

KAREN. I guess...I guess you could say, Marianne, that I am finding everything challenging today.

MARIANNE. Well, I think you are doing very good work here, Karen.

KAREN. Thank you.

MARIANNE. And I know...just how difficult things have been for you.

KAREN. I'm really grateful...

MARIANNE. Nonsense, you deserve this job, Karen. You are a deserving person in spite of any mistakes you've made in your past. We've all made mistakes.

KAREN. I guess...just some days...some days it seems like I've become my mistakes.

MARIANNE. Now that's just a load of hooey.

KAREN. I just feel...so...so...lost, Marianne.

MARIANNE. You come right over here, Missy.

(KAREN *tentatively walks toward* MARIANNE. MARIANNE *gives her a big hug.* KAREN *looks very awkward but lets herself be hugged.* KAREN *begins to sob in* MARIANNE*'s arms.*)

KAREN. I just really want a glass of wine.

MARIANNE. Of course you do. We all get down. We all get down and then want to dance with our demons.

(KAREN *disentangles herself and sniffs a little.* MARIANNE *hands her a tissue.* KAREN *blows her nose really hard.*)

KAREN. Not you, not you, you don't want dance with your demons, Marianne.

MARIANNE. Well Karen. I am a good politician and all good politicians are good actors. Some days...some days....

KAREN. What?

MARIANNE. Some days, let's just say, I feel like doing the "hustle" with my demons.

KAREN. And what…what exactly would doing the "hustle" translate to?

MARIANNE. Now that's neither here nor there.

KAREN. I'm a wino. I love wine, not even good wine – which is particularly sad. I just want that "click" in my head I used to get after my third Big Gulp glass, when things felt warm and fuzzy and nothing much but that very feeling seemed to matter. For me, wine and over-the-counter sleeping pills were my be-all and end-all. It's not hard core but it can still get you into a lot of trouble.

MARIANNE. Believe me, I know how seemingly harmless things can lead you down a destructive path. I know.

KAREN. Really? I mean…Lucille at the life skills center said…

MARIANNE. What exactly did Lucille tell you?

KAREN. Nothing specific, of course. I mean she just said that you believed in giving people a second chance because you had been given one yourself.

MARIANNE. Lucille was right.

KAREN. I guess…I guess I find that fact really comforting. I mean…inspirational too.

MARIANNE. Everything I do Karen, I do to inspire.

KAREN. Wow. That must be exhausting.

MARIANNE. You have a very unique way of looking at things.

KAREN. I'm working on being more positive. I suck at it. Oopsy.

MARIANNE. Positivity is a choice, Karen.

KAREN. I don't buy that. All the positive people I know, seem to have been born with some mysterious Polly-ana gene.

MARIANNE. Not me.

KAREN. Come on. You like wake up singing, "Oh what a beautiful morning." And then jog ten miles.

MARIANNE. I have never jogged so much as a mile in my life. And there was a time, a time when I woke up every morning thinking about my breakfast daiquiri.

KAREN. Uh…was that…your…

MARIANNE. After Susanna died, a part of me died. You could say, my blender and I became best friends. My husband thought I was making health shakes, until I was arrested for shoplifting in a Linens 'N Things in a Mall just north of Savannah three sheets to the wind.

I'd make myself numb in the mornings on strawberry Daiquiris and then pop five Dexatrim to get myself out of the house so I could steal things I didn't need.

I wanted to destroy myself inside and out. But now, now it's all OK, Karen.

KAREN. Really?

MARIANNE. It's OK because I was caught. I wanted to get caught, so someone would stop me. Just like you wanted to be stopped.

KAREN. I'm not sure I wanted to be stopped. I got caught and unless I stopped, I would do prison time, which scared me to death. Isn't that different?

MARIANNE. Is it? I walked out of that Linens 'N Things drunk out of my gourd holding a Hoover I hadn't paid for. If that wasn't a cry for help then what was it?

KAREN. Poor shoplifting technique?

MARIANNE. *(laughing)* You! You have a crackling wit that I truly appreciate. What are you doing this evening, Karen?

KAREN. Uh…I was going to order in, read a little, maybe take a bath.

MARIANNE. Wrong. You are coming home with me and you are going to have some of my husband's fatty French cooking.

KAREN. I…couldn't, Marianne.

MARIANNE. Karen, I won't take no for an answer. It would be irresponsible of me.

KAREN. But...I'm not sure how I feel about chicken with bacon AND apricots. Sweet and savory, a tricky business.

MARIANNE. I am not leaving this office without you. And no worries, our house is a dry house. My husband has his demons too.

KAREN. It'll be a demon festival.

MARIANNE. I'd like to share a meal with you, Karen, in my home. Sometimes, all you need is a home-cooked meal and a little encouragement to get you back on your feet.

KAREN. Sometimes that's just what you need.

MARIANNE. Is that a yes?

KAREN. I guess it is.

MARIANNE. Frank's just gonna eat you up!

(*blackout*)

(Later that night. **KAREN** *at a pay phone.)*

KAREN. Nathan, it's…Peg. I tried to find your home number but there are like fifteen Nathan Friedman's in the Boston/Cambridge area.

Uh…so…I found out some pretty weird stuff about my boss…let's just say the DARKNESS IN HER PAST involves an intense predilection for Daquiris, Dexatrim and dabbling with cleptomania.

So, I called my ex who works at the Post and will do anything for me because…well…after all he is BANGING my kid sister. See the thing is my boss told me that the diet pill/Daquiri habit happened in response to her daughter's death. But the weird thing is…the upsetting thing is: her daughter died *after* she was arrested.

She lied. I can't believe she lied. But she did.

So…I guess I'm in. I'm in. I am in.

(blackout)

ACT TWO

(*JESSICA's office.* **LIZZIE** *sits in a chair and bites her nails.* **JESSICA** *smiles at her.*)

LIZZIE. I guess…I guess…I'm confused.

(*JESSICA smiles at* **LIZZIE** *her smile freezes. She speaks to the audience.*)

JESSICA. I hate my job. I long for evening television and the weekend. I have become like most Americans – who wait for slivers of free time where they space out and forget who they have become.

I am not sure when or where in history work became something that was supposed to be fulfilling. Why is what we choose to do to survive so important?

It wasn't always important to me. Once…once upon a long time ago I was 22 and in love with a beautiful Italian woman named Flavia. She had an ancient, heartbreaking face that I would have happily wasted my life looking at. I followed her to Rome and did the things that you do in a country where you can't work legally and you're way too young to care. Mostly, I loved Flavia – Flavia of the cork screw curls and the cigarette laugh. It never occurred to me that I had a higher purpose or that there was something else that I should be doing to give meaning to my life other than loving Flavia, until she found someone else to love her perfect Italian parts.

None of my Italian friends asked me what I was going to do as I lingered on hoping that Flavia would grow tired of the slinky blond on her arm – people understood. Everyone loved her. One day as I choked on a sob in the Piazza Navona, it occurred to me that I might never stop crying. Flavia would always love

JESSICA. *(cont.)* someone who was not me. And I knew that wherever I went, whatever I did, whomever I loved, no one could be my life like her…that *something* rather than *someone* would have to fill the space that belonged only to her.

I looked the same as I walked toward my apartment in the Campo di Fiori to call my parents to book me a ticket home. But something suddenly hardened in the messy, beating flesh of my 22-year-old heart. I would make meaning in my life in another way. I would get a job because love was too complicated. What I didn't realize is that there is nothing that you do with great love that does not at some point punch you in the stomach. I wish I could have called in sick, especially today. Or run away. I looked up Flavia's number on the Internet today. That's how much I hate my job.

(She turns to LIZZIE.*)*

Tootsie Pop?

LIZZIE. We're not allowed to eat sugar, except on special occasions. Would you classify this as a special occasion?

*(*JESSICA *hands* LIZZIE *a Tootsie Pop.* LIZZIE *unwraps a Tootsie Pop and begins to lick.)*

JESSICA. I know that this must be hard to wrap your head around…

LIZZIE. It's not that hard.

JESSICA. Of course…

LIZZIE. Stuff like this happens all the time.

JESSICA. And it shouldn't.

LIZZIE. But it does.

JESSICA. Believe me, Lizzie, I don't want to live in a world where things like this happen.

LIZZIE. Dream on, Jessica.

JESSICA. Well…yes…yes…I mean things don't change as quickly as I want them to either.

LIZZIE. People change on TV and in books and movies. Real life: different story.

JESSICA. But change is possible, people can change, Lizzie. I wouldn't do what I do if I didn't believe that with all my heart.

LIZZIE. Then you should air the show.

JESSICA. I should, I just don't know if I can.

LIZZIE. Ever notice how Dusty's voice is really squeaky?

JESSICA. The actor's voice is changing.

LIZZIE. Bugs me.

JESSICA. We've been auditioning new Dusty's.

LIZZIE. Bugs A LOT of Petey's friends too.

JESSICA. It's a challenge to find...find someone with the right timbre.

LIZZIE. I wish he wasn't purple. Purple makes me queasy.

JESSICA. We can't just go and change Dusty's color all of a sudden.

LIZZIE. Orange is my favorite color.

JESSICA. Orange...orange is a great color.

LIZZIE. My Dads said I could get orange high tops if I stopped biting my nails.

JESSICA. Great!

LIZZIE. It'd be great if I could stop. See, change IS difficult, Jessica.

JESSICA. I was a nail biter until...very recently.

LIZZIE. How'd you stop?

JESSICA. I don't...remember.

LIZZIE. Maybe you haven't really stopped for good? *(beat)* I totally get that everyone except people who live in big cities or parts of Massachusetts are homophobic. I get that. So wouldn't it be good to teach the other kids that gay families are pretty much like normal families.

JESSICA. I think that would be a great lesson. And it pains me...

LIZZIE. Like you ever notice just how many kid's shows are about sharing? In my experience, the world has gotten a lot more complicated than whether or not you want to share your beach ball with some other kid. Like Dusty has learnt to share with that greedy Bunny about ten thousand times.

JESSICA. That…that is an exaggeration. Spuds is an only child – bunny – bunny/child/ bunny. Sharing is a big kid issue.

LIZZIE. I guess what confuses me the most is: I won a contest…so now does this mean I didn't win?

(LIZZIE *stops sucking her lollipop.*)

JESSICA. Give it to me.

(JESSICA *rolls the half-eaten lollipop in a tissue and throws it away.* NATHAN *peeks in.*)

NATHAN. Lizzie!

LIZZIE. Nathan!

NATHAN. Wow! This is a surprise.

(LIZZIE *runs to* NATHAN *and hugs him. She clings to him for a long time.*)

NATHAN. Hey kiddo. I didn't know you were in town.

LIZZIE. My Dads and Petey are seeing the national tour of Hairspray for the tenth time.

JESSICA. I left a message at Lizzie's house that I wanted to see her and as luck would have it, she was in Boston.

LIZZIE. Anything not to see that fat girl do the twist. Again.

NATHAN. *(pointed to* JESSICA*)* I wish you'd told me.

LIZZIE. Nathan, you can fix all this, right? Like I don't care that much about it but Petey's been telling everyone and they're gonna think he was lying because he makes stuff up, like he said we had two Moms that lived in Alaska and they were going to come and live with us in Great Barrington. And now everyone calls him Eskimo-boy. So, you'll fix this, right?

NATHAN. Yes. Yes I will. I will fix it, Lizzie.

JESSICA. Nathan?

NATHAN. Jessica?

JESSICA. Nathan meant...

NATHAN. That he would fix it.

JESSICA. Nathan doesn't know...

NATHAN. Yes he does. Nathan has a plan that he hasn't told Jessica yet. A secret plan.

JESSICA. Secret plans make Jessica very nervous.

NATHAN. Trust Nathan.

JESSICA. Jessica doesn't want Nathan to make promises he can't keep.

NATHAN. Trust Nathan.

JESSICA. Jessica does trust Nathan but wants to remind him that this is a complicated situation with A LOT of people involved. Prenez guarde.

NATHAN. No comprende.

LIZZIE. She said "be careful" in French.

NATHAN. Don't worry, Jessica.

JESSICA. But I am worried...not worried but concerned. Concerned that you don't cross a line, you shouldn't.

NATHAN. If ever there were a time to be a line crosser, it would be now.

JESSICA. This is obviously a conversation for later.

NATHAN. We can talk in front of Lizzie.

LIZZIE. I've got Tootsie Pop mouth. Can someone get me a glass of water.

(*NATHAN* and *JESSICA* *stare at each other for a long moment.*)

Or direct me to the water fountain. Or the Dixie cup station. Tap is fine. Though my Dads filter everything – even orange juice. Just kidding.

JESSICA. I'll get you some water, Lizzie.

(*JESSICA* *leaves.*)

LIZZIE. She reminds me of this girl in my class. Sue Beavers.

NATHAN. What's Sue like?

LIZZIE. She smiles and winces at the same time. I don't trust people who smile too much.

NATHAN. That's what a producer's job is. They smile even while giving you crushing news.

LIZZIE. I could never be a producer.

NATHAN. I'd kill you if you became a producer.

LIZZIE. But you're a producer.

NATHAN. And look at me.

LIZZIE. I thought of a cool job the other day.

NATHAN. Oh yeah. What?

LIZZIE. I want to be a chef to the astronauts. Like make really good powdered meals so astronauts can eat gourmet in space. Do you think I have to learn to be a regular chef first and then learn to make everything powdered?

NATHAN. Probably.

LIZZIE. Imagine: powdered escargots with garlic sauce? It would look just like a little packet of something, like powdered eggs – or Tang (except not orange) but it would be different without looking different. Pretty cool, right?

NATHAN. Pretty cool.

LIZZIE. AND gourmet. *(beat)* Promise you'll fix this Nathan? For Petey?

NATHAN. Promise. But you have to promise me you'll never ever make me eat powdered escargots.

LIZZIE. Deal.

(They do a deal hand-shake.)

(The Au Bon Pain. **KAREN** *and* **NATHAN** *sit at a table amidst a sea of papers.* **NATHAN** *reads something and almost foams at the mouth.)*

NATHAN. This is…Woah! I mean un-fucking-believable! Countless times! COUNTLESS! She lied. She said the incident was AFTER her daughter died.

*(**NATHAN** reads a little more.)*

She never says point blank that she didn't drink or take Dexatrim BEFORE her daughter died. Not important.

KAREN. I think that's pretty important.

NATHAN. Don't you love the way she refers to her drugged up shoplifting as the "pinnacle of addictive behavior."

KAREN. Well…that's what it was.

NATHAN. Can we bring down the government with this? She is the supposed guardian of morality for kids in America and she may have killed her own child through negligence.

KAREN. Key words in that sentence are MAY HAVE.

NATHAN. What does it take to get you excited?

KAREN. The truth. I find the truth very exciting and elusive.

NATHAN. We live in a time of fiction, Peg. The truth has ceased to matter. Turn on the news on any given night and try to find the truth. And even if there is some grain of truth, it's a partial truth, something is being left out, which makes it pretty close to fiction or a lie.

We have a story here. Some of it may be true, some of it may be speculation but does it really matter? What matters is that someone who professes to lead a highly moral and exemplary life altered the facts of her history to make herself seem a victim of grief and sorrow, when in fact, what she really was, was your garden-variety addict.

KAREN. Good term.

NATHAN. No offence.

(NATHAN *eats some Danish.*)

NATHAN. This isn't bad.

KAREN. *(reading)* Yeah...their baked goods are surprisingly fresh.

NATHAN. I admit...I was biased. I thought there was nothing "Bon" about the "Pain" here.

KAREN. *(looking up)* You have a lot of biases.

NATHAN. Excuse me?

KAREN. *(pointed)* I mean, just because you're a lefty with a bee in your bonnet doesn't mean that you're devoid of biases.

NATHAN. But my biases are right. What...what's going on?

KAREN. I have fewer biases than you – that's what's going on.

NATHAN. How can you possibly know that?

KAREN. Because I am a "garden-variety addict."

NATHAN. I'm sorry, Peg.

KAREN. My name isn't Peg.

NATHAN. If you told me your name, I would be happy to use it.

KAREN. I know about biases because I am white and college educated and I have been on welfare. It takes away a lot of assumptions...assumptions I had about...people.

NATHAN. OK. I get it. But you can't assume to know what I think.

KAREN. OK...I don't know what you think. *(beat)* Truthfully, I don't really want to know. I'm not sure I can handle anyone's thoughts but my own. Everyone's convictions and the history they bring to their convictions and the smallness that really lies behind the big ideas they profess to believe – I find that smallness exhausting.

NATHAN. That's very cynical.

KAREN. Whatever you say Mr. "We live in a time of fiction." Try being like $500,000 in debt, then let's chat about cynicism.

NATHAN. Note taken.

KAREN. Don't be all...

NATHAN. What am I now?

KAREN. Pissy.

NATHAN. I don't know you well enough for you to call me pissy.

KAREN. Look, this is just how I feel – honestly. I'm not all righteous.

NATHAN. I am not "all righteous" either. Ultimately, this is not about me. It's about a little girl who deserves to be heard.

KAREN. And it's about you. You also want to be heard.

NATHAN. Hey! *You* called me! You showed me that crazy memo and then dug up all this dirt on someone who has a master plan to undermine American culture as we know it. Someone who walks and talks the moral high ground while leading a very sketchy life...

KAREN. She LED a sketchy life. It WAS sketchy.

NATHAN. But she lied about it.

KAREN. Sometimes, you have to lie to get a job. You've never fudged on your resume?

NATHAN. I'm not in public office. I mean...God. You? You don't agree with her?

KAREN. Of course not. But I understand her. When your life has been totalled and you have to begin again... you have to believe strongly in something, anything to get up in the morning, anything to stop you from swallowing that omni-present bottle of aspirin...And that "something" can transform into beliefs, heartfelt beliefs... that you hold on to for dear life...because the alternative is death.

NATHAN. So...so...I'm terribly confused.

KAREN. You should be confused.

NATHAN. Do you or do you not want to release this information to your ex at the Post?

KAREN. Marianne Fitzgibbons is not a bad person, even if she did some questionable things in the past...even if I don't believe what she believes...she is still a person with hopes and dreams and deep disappointments. She matters, simply because she is.

NATHAN. Are you...a Buddhist or something?

KAREN. I hate Buddhism. Too hard. Bottom line, if we leak this information, she won't be a person anymore. She'll be a liar, a drunk, a woman who abused her power to cover the truth.

NATHAN. Look I understand that Marianne is human and I deeply appreciate her humanity – I don't know if that's quite true...Sometimes I just wish all the people in this administration had found something beside Jesus to get them through the rough patches. Call me unjust, I care more about Lizzie Goldberg-Jones than Marianne Fitzgibbons

KAREN. Why?

NATHAN. Because she's a good kid with a big heart and I can't bear to disappoint her...because I believe in the infinite possibility of her goodness. Trust me, she is special and most kids leave me cold – my own included.

KAREN. Yikes.

NATHAN. Not always but sometimes. Not Lizzie. She could be the president, or a great third grade teacher to someone who cures cancer. And disappointment chips away at your faith in life, it makes you less...it shrinks your heart. And I don't want anyone to shrink Lizzie's heart.

KAREN. Someone will. It's inevitable.

NATHAN. But I can try and stop this particular disappointment.

KAREN. I guess I'm not positive children are the future.

NATHAN. You should meet this kid.

KAREN. All kids are selfish.

NATHAN. True. My kids often sadden me.

KAREN. I worry about your children.

NATHAN. They're fine. Great. Whatever. Look, I make programming for kids – sometimes knowing that it will do
nothing to save them from their own inevitable medi-
ocrity. But there are remarkable kids and they should
be encouraged and held up for the world to see.

KAREN. Spend some time with *your* kids, Nathan. Let
Lizzie's parents worry about her.

(A moment. NATHAN *takes this in.)*

NATHAN. So…you actually like Marianne?

KAREN. It's weird.

NATHAN. How? Tell me how it's weird.

KAREN. I get her. And I want her story. It's like a movie…
things were OK for her, then they got truly miserable,
and then they got amazing again.

NATHAN. You like happy endings…who doesn't like a
happy ending, Peg?

KAREN. My name is Karen Marie Wilohodjian.

NATHAN. Wilo…Wilo…

KAREN. Wilohodjian. It's Armenian. I'm half Armenian.

NATHAN. Think about Lizzie's story, Karen Marie Wilohodjian.

KAREN. Lizzie has years and years to recover. There's no
fourth act for Marianne.

(a pause)

NATHAN. So…I don't…I don't know where we stand.

KAREN. I need to talk to her.

NATHAN. When? When exactly? Your boss is trying with all
her Christian might to cancel Dusty, not just the gay
Daddy episode – the ENTIRE show. So when, Karen,
when are you gonna sit down and have a chin wag with
Marianne? After Sesame Street is off the air and Itsy
Bitsy Jesus is all the rage?

KAREN. I need to find out what really happened, Nathan.

NATHAN. And you honestly think she'll tell you?

KAREN. Yes.

(lights down)

*(**MARIANNE**'s office a few days later. **JESSICA** sits opposite **MARIANNE** with her mouth open. A long moment.)*

JESSICA. I can't. I can't. I can't.

MARIANNE. You must see my point?

JESSICA. But. But. But. But

MARIANNE. You must understand.

JESSICA. I don't understand. It's like…like…killing off Lucille Ball…

MARIANNE. You know, you know at some level I am right.

JESSICA. Or bludgeoning Andy Griffith…

MARIANNE. Now, no need for theatrics, Jessica.

JESSICA. Not a good analogy…Murdering Snoopy! That's what this is like. You are…a…a…a…

MARIANNE. What am I?

JESSICA. A Snoopy assassin!

MARIANNE. But I love Snoopy.

JESSICA. Don't you see, canceling Dusty is like killing Snoopy. But I said, I said more than once in writing that I wouldn't air the Goldberg-Jones episode. Maybe in New York or San Francisco, if local member stations insist. I gave my word, my word is everything. I have…I have sacrificed, things…principles, things that matter to me to make this work…to find some common ground.

MARIANNE. You are no spring chicken, Jessica.

JESSICA. I don't…I just don't know how to respond to that.

MARIANNE. You are old enough to know that sometimes you just gotta take a deep breath in, let go, then MOVE ON…

JESSICA. But Dusty…I…we…we have seven Emmys and a Peabody. We won a Peabody…You can't cancel a show that won a Peabody.

MARIANNE. You seem confused about your job description, Jessica, you're not in a position to tell me what I can or cannot do. *(beat)* Let me spell it out for ya: I can do whatever I want. Git it?

JESSICA. No. I don't GIT it. Dusty teaches kids to be good human beings. Do you know how hard it is to learn to be vaguely human in this insane time we're living in?

MARIANNE. You took government money, Jessica and used it to further a specific agenda, an agenda that we feel is not appropriate for young children. End of story. End of funding.

JESSICA. Have you ever even met someone gay?

MARIANNE. That is neither here nor there.

JESSICA. I'd say it's right here, right in this room, staring at right you.

MARIANNE. I see.

JESSICA. And what do you see, Marianne? We shook hands. We talked about the weather. You crushed my dreams. I grovelled. And all the while I was one of THEM. You just can't wrap your head around it. I seem so normal.

MARIANNE. Not my version of normal.

JESSICA. Your version of normal disgusts me.

(MARIANNE *speaks into the intercom.*)

MARIANNE. Karen, would you be a honey and show Ms. Fields out.

KAREN. *(V.O.)* There is someone here to see you. Some… well…people.

(KAREN *enters with* LIZZIE *and* NATHAN.)

KAREN. I have no idea how they got past security.

LIZZIE. One of my Dads founded Act Up, that's how. I'm Lizzie Goldberg-Jones.

MARIANNE. Nice to meet you, Lizzie. I am always so pleased to meet resourceful young people.

JESSICA. Nathan. Not a good idea.

KAREN. Such a bad idea.

NATHAN. I can't just stand by anymore.

LIZZIE. So…OK. LISTEN UP! Bottom line, you have to air the show.

MARIANNE. Well...Lizzie. I would like to because when I watched the episode I was struck by what a great kid you are.

LIZZIE. I'm not leaving until you promise me in WRITING and we get the promise NOTARIZED.

MARIANNE. Aren't you something? So intelligent and passionate.

NATHAN. Puh-lease. Don't even try buttering her up.

JESSICA. Nathan, it's no use. Believe me.

NATHAN. I'm tired of being diplomatic and cautious. It doesn't work.

MARIANNE. I too am weary of being cautious and that is why we are canceling Dusty, or at least withdrawing government funding from the show altogether, which as far as I can see means the show will not air, in any market, anywhere, any time in the near future.

NATHAN. You're canceling Dusty? Fuck!

MARIANNE. You must be one of Lizzie's "Dads"?

NATHAN. No. I am not...but it would be fine if I were.

LIZZIE. *(to MARIANNE)* You're canceling the show? How can you do that? *(to JESSICA)* Can she do that?

JESSICA. She can do anything 'cause God is on her side.

LIZZIE. God told you to cancel the show?

MARIANNE. I'd prefer if we kept the Lord out of this.

NATHAN. Fine by me. I don't want the Lord on my TV either.

MARIANNE. I meant, out of this conversation.

NATHAN. Are you even capable of not feeling "blessed" or moved by "God's love" for a nanosecond?

MARIANNE. Karen, call security.

KAREN. Oh...OK...OK...Yeah sure.

(KAREN *picks up the phone.*)

NATHAN. Put down the phone, Karen. You want to put it down, I know you do.

MARIANNE. How could you possibly presume to know what she wants? Security ASAP, Karen.

NATHAN. *(to KAREN)* Tell her! *(beat)* This is your moment. Let it rip, Karen Marie Wilohodgian.

MARIANNE. Karen, do you know this…man?

KAREN. Sort of. He's a producer on Dusty.

MARIANNE. I see.

KAREN. Uh…Marianne…I…have been meaning to talk to you about some uh things…that I uh…have been on my…uh…well…my…

LIZZIE. *(to MARIANNE)* Did you have a vision?

MARIANNE. What do you mean, honey?

LIZZIE. Like the Buddha had visions under the Bodhi tree and came up with the four noble truths.

MARIANNE. I'm afraid I'm a little rusty when it comes to the Buddha.

LIZZIE. So, did you have some kind of vision that told you that animated dust balls were evil and shouldn't visit gay families because they're evil too?

NATHAN. Any visions, Marianne? Maybe a prophetic dream?

KAREN. Nathan…don't…just don't.

MARIANNE. This is not the time or place to discuss my faith and how that faith manifests itself in the choices I make in my work.

NATHAN. No visions, Lizzie.

JESSICA. I have a bad feeling. Let's get out of here.

LIZZIE. But…some strong emotion makes you think this is the right thing to do.

MARIANNE. That's a great way of putting it. You are not to blame, Lizzie. Your "Dads" chose their lifestyle not you. And I don't want you or your brother to think that we are judging you.

LIZZIE. But by not airing the show you are judging me. Duh?

NATHAN. Duh?

KAREN. Marianne, I mean…Lizzie does have a point.

MARIANNE. Karen, I am very unclear as to why you have not called security.

KAREN. Because…uh…I've been…well…uh. I think…

NATHAN. Tell her, Karen!

KAREN. *(to* NATHAN*)* Lay off, OK?

MARIANNE. I'm sorry you feel judged, Lizzie. That was certainly not my intention.

LIZZIE. Then air my episode.

MARIANNE. Let me ask you this, it's something I have long been curious about, if you could have a more traditional family, would you?

JESSICA. Time to go back to Cambridge where it's safe.

KAREN. Good idea. Everybody should leave. *(beat)* I am calling security. Watch me dial.

(**KAREN** *picks up the phone. She dials.*)

LIZZIE. I'm not going anywhere.

NATHAN. Me neither.

JESSICA. Come on, Nathan.

NATHAN. I'm not like you, Jessica.

JESSICA. What do you mean by that?

NATHAN. You know what I mean.

JESSICA. Use your words. You're a writer for God's sake.

NATHAN. If I were you, I couldn't turn my back on this.

JESSICA. Because I'm a producer of Dusty? Or because I'm gay.

NATHAN. That's not a question I can answer.

JESSICA. Because I have sex with women does not mean I have to be political in ways that you deem appropriate.

NATHAN. I think you're wrong there.

JESSICA. I don't think it's for you to dictate to me what is right or wrong about my behavior in relation to my sexual orientation.

NATHAN. Your lack of empathy in this situation has been astounding and unfathomable to me.

JESSICA. Fuck You! You self-righteous asshole.

(*The following lines should all overlap.*)

MARIANNE. Security. Karen, we/really need security.

KAREN. //They have me on hold!!!

NATHAN. I am not self-righteous. You don't have a single feeling in your frozen, fucked up heart.

JESSICA. Please, you are a poster boy for self-righteous martyrdom. You're just waiting for any situation to be outraged about. You're a child.

NATHAN. Well, you're a cold-hearted bitch who needs to get laid.

(**LIZZIE** *stands up in the chair and waves her arms.*)

LIZZIE. EVERYONE OUT!

MARIANNE. What has the world come to when a child is the only voice of reason in a room full of adults?

(**KAREN** *puts down the phone.*)

KAREN. (*almost in tears*) I...I...can't get a PERSON!

LIZZIE. I'd like to speak to Marianne alone, please.

JESSICA. I don't know if that's a good idea, Lizzie.

MARIANNE. I think it's the best idea I've heard all day.

NATHAN. There is no way I am leaving you with this...ghoul dressed up as Glenda the good witch.

(**NATHAN** *and* **LIZZIE** *look at each other.*)

LIZZIE. Please. Please, Nathan.

NATHAN. I'll be right outside the door. And I am ready to break it down if you play dirty with this child.

MARIANNE. I am not the one swearing in front of minors.

NATHAN. I know all about you and how you treat minors. Ask her about Susanna, Lizzie.

MARIANNE. Don't you dare utter my daughter's name.

NATHAN. What happened to your daughter on September 10th, 1993 at approximately 1:45 p.m.? Where were you, Marianne, when your daughter fell off the monkey bars and hit her head so hard she died from inter-cranial hemorrhaging?

MARIANNE. I will have you arrested if you continue on like this.

NATHAN. Maybe, just maybe, you were getting your afternoon high on and didn't see your little six-year-old girl climbing to her death?

JESSICA. She killed her daughter?

NATHAN. We can't get her on murder but manslaughter is a definite possibility.

MARIANNE. Your speculations about my past are of no consequence to me.

NATHAN. Oh! There are going to be consequences, CNN consequences.

LIZZIE. I NEED to speak to Marianne.

KAREN. Will somebody please just listen to Lizzie!

NATHAN. What's it feel like to be OVER, Marianne?

MARIANNE. I haven't even begun. You can't just be angry because you don't like what I think. You have to have a clearly articulated agenda of your own.

NATHAN. My agenda is, and I hope this is articulate enough, to keep you away from deciding a fucking thing about what children should and shouldn't know. Forever.

MARIANNE. That's an impulsive reaction, I wouldn't exactly describe it as a defined ideology. It's where we get you every time.

(KAREN *is on the phone.*)

KAREN. Hey security, how you doin'? Been trying to get through. *(She looks around.)* Let me see if I still need you.

(NATHAN *walks to the door.*)

I think we're safe.

(KAREN *hangs up.* NATHAN *turns around.*)

NATHAN. *(to* MARIANNE*)* See you on the evening news.

MARIANNE. I can't tell you how much I am looking forward to that.

NATHAN. Ditto.

(*NATHAN exits.* **JESSICA** *begins to leave. She turns around.*)

JESSICA. I'm sorry Lizzie, so sorry. Tell your Dads that for me?

(**LIZZIE** *turns away from* **JESSICA.**)

I've never been very political. I like stories more than politics. We made great stories Marianne.

(**JESSICA** *exits.*)

KAREN. I should go.

LIZZIE. You can stay.

MARIANNE. Lizzie, I'm sorry that you have had to witness so much unpleasantness. We should protect children from the chaos of adult's cruelty.

LIZZIE. Tricky, that.

(**LIZZIE** *picks up the picture of Susanna.*)

LIZZIE. Is this your daughter?

MARIANNE. Yes. She was six when she left us. She'd be almost all grown up now.

LIZZIE. Sad.

MARIANNE. Isn't a day that goes by where I don't miss her.

LIZZIE. Our pug Cher died last year. We had a funeral and buried her underneath the morning glorys. My Dads couldn't stop crying, they had Cher before me and Petey.

MARIANNE. Loss is not easy for anyone.

LIZZIE. I bet losing a kid is worse than losing a pug. (*looking at the photo*) She was pretty.

MARIANNE. Wasn't she? Her eyelashes were so long. I threatened to comb 'em, when she was bad. What did you want to talk to me about, Lizzie?

LIZZIE. Sometimes, I think about my biological Mom.

MARIANNE. Course you do. It's natural.

LIZZIE. She put me up for adoption, so I guess she didn't want me around.

MARIANNE. Maybe it was impossible for her to have you around. She wanted the best for you.

LIZZIE. Do you think I got the best?

MARIANNE. Well...you seem like a great kid.

LIZZIE. Sometimes, I do wish my family was more traditional.

MARIANNE. Of course you do, honey.

LIZZIE. Nobody signs on to be an outsider. I mean, maybe like if you're born a Goth or something. But sure...I think about a Mom who tells me all about her bad perms and dumb dates. That sounds good to me, I'm not gonna lie. But for some reason I didn't get that. I got something more complicated but it doesn't mean it's wrong.

MARIANNE. I never said it was wrong, Lizzie.

KAREN. You kinda did. I mean, not in so many words, but her Dads' choices, they aren't right in your mind?

MARIANNE. *(pointed)* Karen, I'm surprised at your line of questioning, particularly as you are a representative of this office.

KAREN. No I just...I just think it's important to be clear here. It's just she thinks that you think her life is somehow wrong and it's all so complicated...like Lizzie said. It's complicated but everyone tries to make it simple.

MARIANNE. What are you getting at, Karen?

KAREN. Marianne, I admire you in this way that is hard to describe to other people who haven't started their lives over. So...I admire you and at the same time I just wish you were more truthful.

MARIANNE. About what exactly, Karen?

KAREN. Well. It seems...from some information that I have gathered from a reliable source at the Washington Post and through various public records that you perhaps were not completely truthful about the death of your daughter. I mean the chronology of your drinking and pill-taking is off.

MARIANNE. So, you've been doing a little research paper on me?

KAREN. How can you stand in judgment of Lizzie and her Dads when from what I believe to be true, you've lied about your personal history.

MARIANNE. This is neither the time nor place to discuss this.

KAREN. But her Dads didn't lie. And yet you don't think them worthy of airtime. And you've lied and lied and you're on TV all the time.

LIZZIE. My Dads are honest people. They're even married. We moved to Massachusetts so it would be legal.

MARIANNE. You're just hearing one side of the story, Lizzie.

KAREN. But what's the truth? The truth matters. It has to.

LIZZIE. My Dads are good people.

MARIANNE. I don't doubt that. Good people can make bad choices, happens every day. Your Dads made choices that most God-fearing people think are not right.

KAREN. We're done here, Lizzie. So done.

(KAREN *holds out her hand to* LIZZIE. LIZZIE *walks to the door and turns around.*)

LIZZIE. Petey and I wanted to be on Dusty more than anything else in the world.

MARIANNE. Everyone wants to be on TV, honey.

(KAREN *walks* LIZZIE *out of the office.* MARIANNE *picks up the phone and dials.*)

MARIANNE. Hey Holly-Louise, Marianne Fitzgibbons here. Tell the press secretary to call me as soon as she gets out of the briefing. It's a code red.

(MARIANNE *puts down the phone. She kneels at her desk and prays.* KAREN *enters.* MARIANNE *sees* KAREN *and stands up. A silence.*)

MARIANNE. Great kid.

KAREN. Yeah.

(*a silence*)

(*MARIANNE gestures for* **KAREN** *to come to her. She tentatively steps toward her.* **MARIANNE** *gives her a big hug.*)

MARIANNE. God sent me a gift in you.

KAREN. How? How am I a gift?

MARIANNE. You are a truth seeker. God wanted me to reveal my truth. It's time. *(beat)* I like you, Karen.

KAREN. You don't have to…

MARIANNE. But I really do like you. But if you have not left the building in five minutes, security will escort you to your car. Do not take any files, correspondence, or any written matter of any kind from this office with you. Any personal effects you leave behind will be mailed to you in a timely fashion. And remember to turn in your ID, you don't have a view of the Capitol anymore.

(**KAREN** *begins to leave. She turns around.*)

KAREN. Marianne, what happened with Susanna?

MARIANNE. You'll just have to wait for the evening news, now won't you.

(blackout)

(The flash of cameras. The din of journalists. **MARI-ANNE** *steps to a microphone and shields her eyes.)*

MARIANNE. I have a prepared statement, afterwards if time allows I'll take a few questions

I had a daughter. She died an accidental death. I also had an addiction. These two very painful facts of my life are not related. They are parallel pains. They existed side by side. In the telling of my story, I may well have implied that my addiction to alcohol and over the counter diet aids was related to the death of my daughter – and that was not a lie. After her accidental death in a playground I drank more, I took more pills – I grew farther away from the person I once was. My daughter did not die because I was an alcoholic but her short life may well have been a happier place were I not an addict. The two have nothing to do with one another as my political opponents would have you believe.

I knew my past was a liability when I accepted my job but I also knew that all I had endured, all the strength I had found through God and the kindness my family had bestowed on me would enable me to face whatever came my way. I was prepared because I have suffered greater losses and seen the other side of darkness. It is impossible to return to despair when you know what the true nature of salvation is.

I am fully aware that the vagaries of partisan politics may force me to resign but it does not worry me. What troubles me is our times, where nothing is sacred, where tragedy is turned into scandal, where private pain must be made public at all costs.

I would ask that all of you remember I had a daughter and no longer do and my life will never be the same for that fact. The rest is conjecture that muddies the truth of my most private pain.

Any questions?

(Spot out on **MARIANNE.***)*

NATHAN. Fuck! She was good, her hair was bad but she was good.

KAREN. She spun the story.

NATHAN. How...how...how...did she do that?

KAREN. She believes her own spin. It's a powerful weapon.

NATHAN. These people are made of Teflon. Nothing sticks to them.

KAREN. It will, eventually.

NATHAN. I'm not sure the truth will ever matter again.

KAREN. It has to matter.

NATHAN. She is the villain, right?

KAREN. She's a liar. I'm not sure there are any villains, Nathan.

NATHAN. Ok. I officially give up. You confound me. You play every side of the field. It makes me migrainish.

KAREN. That's my goal in life, to inspire bone crushing headaches in others. *(beat)* You speak to Lizzie?

NATHAN. She won't return my calls. Am I a fool Karen Marie Wilohodjian?

KAREN. Yes.

NATHAN. Gee, thanks.

KAREN. But we need Don Quixotes to stab at windmills and muddle through.

NATHAN. If I'm Don Quixote...are you my Sancho Panza?

KAREN. No. I'm just someone who needs a job. I'm not exactly employable.

NATHAN. Makes two of us.

KAREN. Thanks, Nathan.

NATHAN. For what?

KAREN. Stabbing the windmill.

(blackout)

(A few weeks later. **LIZZIE** *swings on a swing.* **KAREN** *enters.)*

KAREN. Hey. Your Dads told me you were out here.

*(***LIZZIE*** *turns to look at her. She turns away and swings.)*

You probably don't even remember me.

LIZZIE. I remember you. *(long beat, more swinging)* What are you doing here?

KAREN. I was driving around…

LIZZIE. I hate driving around. I get car sick.

*(***KAREN*** *looks around.)*

KAREN. Nice out here. Is it alright if I sit?

LIZZIE. I guess.

*(***KAREN*** *sits on another swing.)*

LIZZIE. Careful of the ropes on that swing, they can give you splinters.

*(***KAREN*** *begins to swing a little.)*

KAREN. I read something interesting recently. Apparently in the bible, there are six warnings to homosexuals and like 362 to heterosexuals. I guess that doesn't mean that God hates heterosexuals more. He must just think they need more supervision…which is probably true…

*(***LIZZIE*** *turns toward her.)*

LIZZIE. Do you think I can pull off orange?

KAREN. What are we talking here? Pants, shirt, a dress?

LIZZIE. A dress. My Dads think orange only works on people with dark skin.

KAREN. If you wear orange, you're definitely going to stand out. Orange is a statement color: I'm here, DEAL with it. Not my idea of a good time but…

LIZZIE. I'm really into this orange sun dress at Express. I think about it all the time. If I had that dress everything would be different.

KAREN. That's asking an awful lot of a piece of clothing.

LIZZIE. I'm gonna get it. Definitely.

(More swinging. LIZZIE *swings pretty high.)*

KAREN. So, I made this list of people, people I think are cool.

LIZZIE. I think Sponge Bob is cool.

KAREN. I am with you, Sponge Bob cool, way cool, he's on my list. Anyhoo, a lot of the people on my list are dead, animated, or live in LA.

LIZZIE. Who's on your list?

KAREN. It's a long list *(*KAREN *takes out her list.)* ...um you know, Ghandi, Betty Boop, Coco Chanel, Martin Luther King, Ray and Charles Eames, Virginia Woolf, Cary Grant, Keith Richards – not dead but looks like he is, Harriet Tubman, George Clooney, Chrissie Hynde from the Pretenders (you have no idea who that is, God I'm old), Bono, Pedro Almodovar, Bugs Bunny, Mickey Mouse, Kermit, Sponge Bob AND Gary his pet snail and...you.

LIZZIE. *I'm* on your list?

*(*KAREN *gives* LIZZIE *the list.)*

KAREN. I think you're cool Lizzie. *(beat)* And I wasn't just driving around. I came here today to tell you that.

*(*LIZZIE *swings some more.)*

LIZZIE. My favorite one is Leviticus 20:13 "If a man lies with a man as one lies with a woman, both of them have done what is detestable. They must be put to death; their blood will be on their own heads." Detestable is what my English teacher Ms. Lippman would call a "forceful adjective."

KAREN. Lizzie, you can't let the bible get you down.

LIZZIE. I don't. But my Dads are always saying that the best way to fight prejudice is to try and understand what the people who hate you are afraid of.

KAREN. I wish that I'd had like one of your dads...part time even.

LIZZIE. After the show aired – they only aired it in Massachusetts and Vermont – we were kind of famous. Someone asked for Petey's autograph outside of Lowe's. And this family of Lesbians in Amherst took our picture when we were getting pizza. And in the picture my Dads looked really proud and Petey looked genuinely happy because he usually has this look like he just smelt cat poo. But he was smiling because people saw us as special because we were on TV, not just because we're a gay family. And I was glad for a while.

KAREN. Just awhile?

LIZZIE. Folks have short memories and then they canceled the show. And that stupid Marianne is like on the cover of every magazine with her weirdo hairdo. And nothing really changed.

KAREN. Sucks.

LIZZIE. Pretty much.

(the two swing some more)

LIZZIE. Did you get fired?

KAREN. Yup. It wasn't the right job for me. Washington isn't the right place for me either. I'm thinking about moving.

LIZZIE. I'd like to move to Buenos Aires. Gay marriage is legal there and everyone is beautiful and has a lot of therapy and plastic surgery. Last year at day camp there was a counselor from Buenos Aires, I don't think he'd had plastic surgery. His name was Eduardo. Everyone was in love with him.

KAREN. What did you think of Eduardo?

LIZZIE. He was pretty cool, I guess. He taught tennis. I liked to watch him play. He looked...well...kinda hot when he played, you know really confident and tanned. But he didn't have any hair on his legs. My friend Ramona and I wondered about that a lot.

KAREN. Sounds like you were crushing on him.

LIZZIE. Whatever. Do you have like a new job?

KAREN. Uh...no. I'm trying to figure out the next step. Sometimes, it seems like I'm always trying to figure out the next step.

LIZZIE. I know the Friendly's in Pittsfield is hiring.

KAREN. Perhaps Friendly's is my destiny.

LIZZIE. You don't really look like someone who works in Friendly's.

KAREN. Thanks.

(They both swing.)

Look, wherever I end up, maybe we could figure out a way to hang out sometimes? If you want to? Or you could call me, or e-mail me? And you can ask me anything that you don't feel comfortable asking your Dads. Nothing shocks me. But I warn you, Lizzie, I could give you terrible advice. I have made a hash of my life. A hash. But I need to believe there is a reason horrible things happen to great people and the wrong people win and that somehow something lovely and good can emerge out of the ashes. I need that.

(Some more swinging.)

LIZZIE. I get it.

KAREN. Yeah.

LIZZIE. Yeah.

(The two swing in silence.)

End of Play

Also by
Cusi Cram...

Fuente

Lucy and the Conquest

A Lifetime Burning

Please visit our website **samuelfrench.com** for complete
descriptions and licensing information.

MORE CUSI CRAM FROM SAMUEL FRENCH

FUENTE

Cusi Cram

Dramatic Comedy / 3m, 4f

Something is not right. There is a secret humidity in the air in a town where the breezes have been on strike for two hundred years. Soledad thinks she is Alexis Carrington from *Dynasty* and feels itchy. Chaparro can't seem to scratch her itch anymore. Esteban might just be the man for the job. And Adela watches it all unfold as if it were a soap opera on TV. Maybe it is? Anything is possible in Fuente, an almost-real town, somewhere between where North America ends and South America begins.

Fuente is a magically-real comedy set in a remote desert town about love, revenge, escape, and the perilous powers of Aqua Net hairspray.

"The play, *Fuente*, is powerful, moving and original, which after a three-year development process and a Herrick Theatre Foundation Prize for New Play, is being given a smartly staged, well acted world premiere at Boyd's smaller venue in Sheffield.

"Cram has written a small-scale at once real and mythical epic about love, vengeance and one's sense of place. The language is earthy and poetic. The characters and their stories are sad but also funny enough to have the audience burst out laughing. The Garcia Marquez-like magic is amusingly propelled by a bottle of Aqua Net hair spray." - CurtainUp.com